DATE DUE		

HISTORY SPEAKS
PICTURE BOOKS PLUS READER'S THEATER

George Washington and
THE STORY OF THE
U.S. CONSTITUTION

BY **CANDICE RANSOM**

ILLUSTRATED BY **JENI REEVES**

M MILLBROOK PRESS / MINNEAPOLIS

For Ellie Bell —CR

For my aunt, Noreen Black, a "founding"
influence on me —JR

Text copyright © 2011 by Candice Ransom
Illustrations © 2011 by Lerner Publishing Group, Inc.

Millbrook Press
A division of Lerner Publishing Group, Inc.
241 First Avenue North
Minneapolis, MN 55401 U.S.A.

Website address: www.lernerbooks.com

The illustrator thanks Historian Coxe Toogood of Independence National
Historical Park, Archivist Dona McDermott of Valley Forge National Historical
Park, and Collections Manager Adele Barbato of the Bostonian Society for their
expertise in pinpointing the period. Special thanks to models Kory Karamour,
Stuart Reeves, Tegan Croninger, and Justin Croninger.

The image in this book is used with the permission of: © Joseph Sohm/Visions of
America, LLC/Alamy, p. 33.

Library of Congress Cataloging-in-Publication Data

Ransom, Candice F., 1952–
    George Washington and the story of the U.S. Constitution / by Candice
Ransom ; illustrated by Jeni Reeves.
        p.   cm. — (History speaks: picture books plus reader's theater)
    Includes bibliographical references.
    ISBN: 978-0-7613-5877-0 (lib. bdg. : alk. paper)
    1. Washington, George, 1732-1799—Juvenile literature. 2. United
States. Constitutional Convention (1787)—Juvenile literature. 3. United
States. Constitution—Juvenile literature. 4. United States—Politics and
government—1783-1789—Juvenile literature. 5. Constitutional history—
United States—Juvenile literature. I. Reeves, Jeni, ill. II. Title.
E303.R35 2011
973.4—dc22   2010028710

Manufactured in the United States of America
1 – CG – 12/31/10

CONTENTS

George Washington and
the Story of the U.S. Constitution 4

Author's Note 32

Performing Reader's Theater 34

Cast of Characters 36

The Script 37

    Pronunciation Guide 45

    Glossary 45

    Selected Bibliography 46

    Further Reading and Websites 46

    A Note for Teachers and Librarians 48

PHILADELPHIA, PENNSYLVANIA

◆ *May 1787* ◆

They had come to the East Room of the Pennsylvania State House for an important meeting. They promised not to tell anyone what they talked about until they were done.

The men were delegates. They came from nearly all of the thirteen states. A few delegates, like George Washington and Benjamin Franklin, were famous. Seventeen more men were coming. Most had to ride for hundreds of miles on horseback or in carriages.

General George Washington sat in a special chair. He had been the leader of the army during the Revolutionary War. People trusted him. The members elected him to be president of the convention.

The United States was a new country. In 1776, the thirteen colonies had declared independence from Great Britain. Britain's King George III sent troops to fight the colonists. The Americans won.

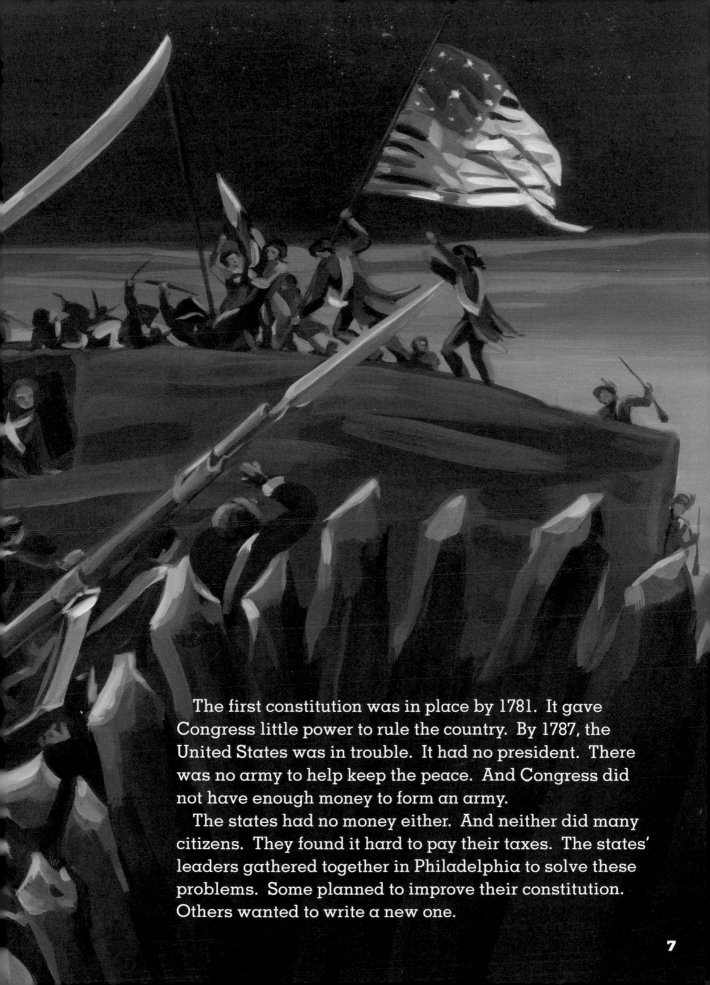

The first constitution was in place by 1781. It gave Congress little power to rule the country. By 1787, the United States was in trouble. It had no president. There was no army to help keep the peace. And Congress did not have enough money to form an army.

The states had no money either. And neither did many citizens. They found it hard to pay their taxes. The states' leaders gathered together in Philadelphia to solve these problems. Some planned to improve their constitution. Others wanted to write a new one.

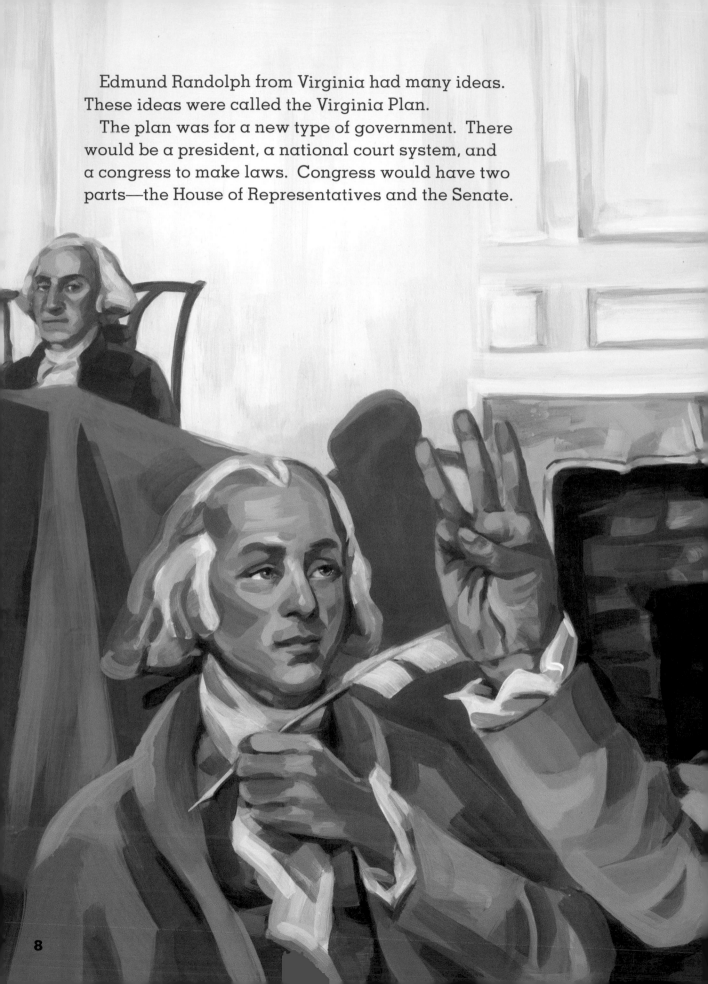

Edmund Randolph from Virginia had many ideas. These ideas were called the Virginia Plan.

The plan was for a new type of government. There would be a president, a national court system, and a congress to make laws. Congress would have two parts—the House of Representatives and the Senate.

Some members worried. Would the president act like a king? Who would elect him? How long should he serve? Alexander Hamilton thought the president should serve for life.

Charles Pinckney from South Carolina asked, "Does the plan get rid of state governments?" The delegates began to argue. At the time, each state had one vote in Congress. Under the new plan, things would be different. The number of votes each state had would be based on how many people lived there. The small states had fewer people than the big states. They were afraid the big states would run the country.

James Madison, from Virginia, sat up front.
He took notes as the members debated.

The small states had a different plan. They called it the New Jersey Plan. Congress would only have one group of representatives. The states would keep their equal number of votes.

Most of the delegates did not like the New Jersey Plan. They thought the Virginia Plan would work better. But they wanted to make changes to it.

Elbridge Gerry from Massachusetts didn't like one part of the Virginia Plan. He did not want ordinary people to vote for members of the House of Representatives. Gerry said, "[People] have the wildest ideas of government."

The delegates could not go home until their work was done. They would have to stay in Philadelphia all summer.

By June, the weather was very hot. The men wore wool
coats, thick stockings, and heavy shoes. Many also wore
itchy powdered wigs.

Big black flies buzzed around the East Room. The heat
made the flies worse.

When the delegates went for a walk, they often passed the Walnut Street Prison. The prisoners begged them for money. Sometimes the prisoners called them names.

The members talked and voted. But they could not answer the biggest question. Should the large states send more representatives to Congress than the small states?

"Maybe the nation should have thirteen states the same size," said William Paterson of New Jersey.

"Or divide the country into four equal parts," said South Carolina's Charles Pinckney. No one thought much of these ideas.

Day after day, everyone argued. The small states were angry at the large states.

"Gentlemen," said Gunning Bedford from the tiny state of Delaware. "I do not trust you! If the large states take all the power, they will crush the small states."

Would they ever find a way to agree?

The delegates took a break for the Fourth of July.
Church bells rang, and fireworks exploded all across
the country.

In Boston, families watched the fireworks light up the square in front of the Old State House.

The delegates were in a bad mood after the holiday. They were tired of arguing. Benjamin Franklin was afraid some members would quit. He wanted them to understand that they could not get everything they wanted.

"When a carpenter makes a table and the boards do not fit," he told them, "he cuts a little from both boards to make a joint."

Roger Sherman from Connecticut came up with a new plan. It included parts of both the Virginia and New Jersey plans. Citizens would elect members of the House of Representatives. The number of members would be based on the population of the state. Each state would send two representatives to the Senate. Members of the Senate would be chosen by the state governments.

Finally, the delegates agreed. The Connecticut Plan became known as the Great Compromise.

A small group formed to write a draft of the new Constitution. The rest of the delegates took a vacation. George Washington visited Valley Forge. His army had camped there during the Revolutionary War. Now crops were growing in the fields. Washington stayed with friends. He decided to go fishing for trout.

The convention met again. This time, members looked at printed copies of the Constitution. Their work was not done yet.

They decided the president would be elected by people called electors. Voters in each state would choose these electors. The president would serve for four years. If he became sick, the vice president would take over. Congress could make changes to the Constitution when it needed to. These changes would be called amendments.

The Constitution grew longer. The members got new copies with all their changes. They read the inspiring words at the beginning, "We the People of the United States, in Order to form a more perfect Union . . ."

On September 17, 1787, the U.S. Constitution was finished. Thirty-nine delegates signed it.

Benjamin Franklin pointed to George Washington's chair. He said, "I've wondered if the sun carved on the back is rising or setting. Now I know it is a rising sun." A rising sun meant hope for the country's future.

But the delegates still weren't done. The states had to vote on the Constitution. At least nine states had to approve. If not, there would be no new government.

Newspapers printed copies of
the Constitution. People read it and
argued about it. Some thought the new
government would be too powerful.

Mercy Otis Warren was from Massachusetts. She spoke against the Constitution. She thought the president would be too much like a king.

Delaware was the first state to approve the Constitution. New Jersey, Pennsylvania, Georgia, and Connecticut followed. Slowly, more states voted yes. On June 21, 1788, New Hampshire became the ninth state to vote yes. The United States had a new Constitution.

July 4, 1788, was another Independence Day. People were happy about the new Constitution. In Philadelphia, cannons boomed. Soldiers marched down the streets. Crowds cheered at a huge copy of the Constitution. It was on a float pulled by six horses.

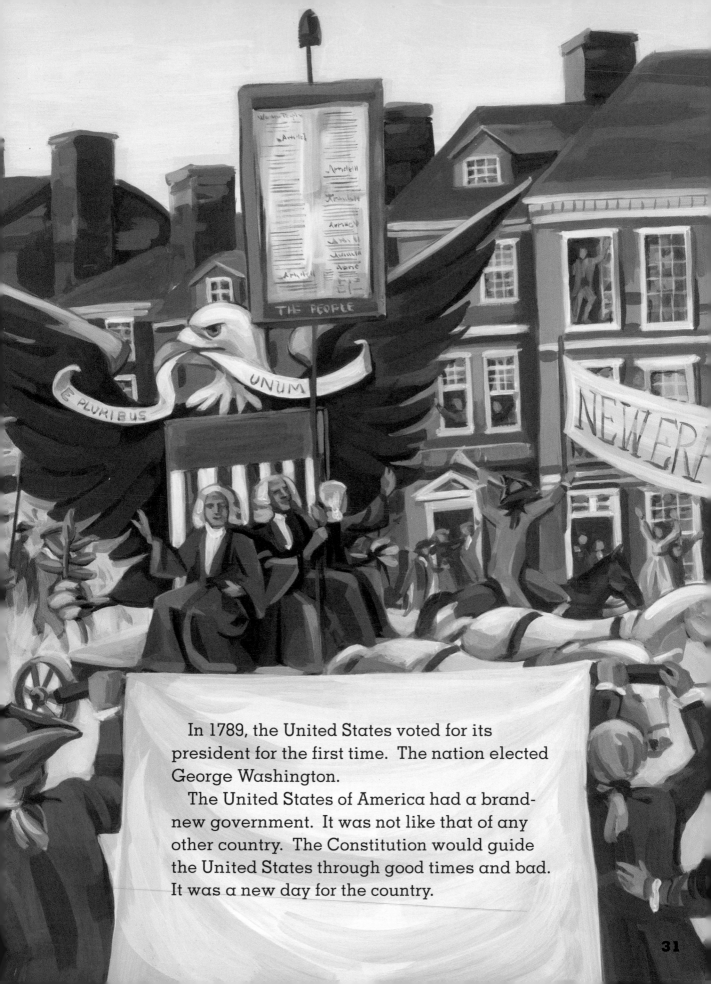

In 1789, the United States voted for its president for the first time. The nation elected George Washington.

The United States of America had a brand-new government. It was not like that of any other country. The Constitution would guide the United States through good times and bad. It was a new day for the country.

Author's Note

In 1781, the United States had its first constitution. Each state made its own laws. In some ways, they acted like small countries. Congress could declare war against another nation. But it had no money to raise an army.

The Revolutionary War had lasted for seven years. Congress had spent a lot of money on food, clothing, and supplies for the troops. After the war, Congress wanted the states to pay back this money. The government asked the states to pay taxes. But it couldn't force them to pay. The new nation needed a stronger government.

Fifty-five men went to Philadelphia. They came from New Hampshire, Connecticut, Massachusetts, New York, New Jersey, Delaware, Pennsylvania, Maryland, Virginia, North Carolina, South Carolina, and Georgia. Only Rhode Island did not send a representative. Rhode Island was afraid of a strong national government.

James Madison attended the convention every day. His notes have helped us understand what happened that summer. I have used Madison's notes to create the discussions in this story.

George Mason, Elbridge Gerry, and Edmund Randolph did not sign the Constitution. They believed it needed a special set of laws to protect people. They called these laws the Bill of Rights. The three delegates wanted to guarantee Americans' rights to free speech, fair trials, and freedom of religion, for example.

THE CHAIR OF GEORGE WASHINGTON IN THE RESTORED EAST ROOM IN PHILADELPHIA, PENNSYLVANIA

Newspapers reprinted the new Constitution so that people could read it. But James Madison, Alexander Hamilton, and John Jay wanted to help them understand it. They wrote pamphlets explaining how the Constitution worked.

After the states approved the Constitution, the Bill of Rights was added. It became the first ten amendments.

The Constitution has twenty-seven amendments. The Thirteenth Amendment banned slavery. The states approved it in 1865. In 1911, the Seventeenth Amendment let people elect Senate members. In 1920, the Nineteenth Amendment gave women the right to vote.

The U.S. Constitution is one of the oldest written constitutions still being used by any country in the world. Visitors to Washington, D.C., can see the original document. It is on display in the National Archives Building. George Washington's chair still sits in the State House in Philadelphia. That building was renamed Independence Hall.

Performing Reader's Theater

Dear Student,

Reader's Theater is a dramatic reading. It is a little like a play, but you don't need to memorize your lines. Here are some tips that will help you do your best in a Reader's Theater performance.

BEFORE THE PERFORMANCE

- **Choose your part:** Your teacher may assign parts, or you may be allowed to choose your own part. The character you play does not need to be the same age as you. A boy can play the part of a girl, and a girl can play the part of a boy. That's why it's called acting!

- **Find your lines:** Your character's name is always the same color. The name at the bottom of each page tells you which character has the first line on the next page. If you are allowed to write on your script, highlight your lines. If you cannot write on the script, you may want to use sticky flags to mark your lines.

- **Check pronunciations of words:** If your character's lines include any words you aren't sure how to pronounce, check the pronunciation guide on page 45. If a word isn't there or you still aren't sure how to say it, check a dictionary or ask a teacher, librarian, or other adult.

- **Use your emotions:** Think about how your character feels in the story. If you imagine how your character feels, the audience will hear the emotion in your voice.

- **Use your imagination:** Think about how your character's voice might sound. For example, an old man's voice will sound different from a baby's voice. If you do change your voice, make sure the audience can still understand the words you are saying.

- **Practice your lines:** Even though you do not need to memorize your lines, you should still be comfortable reading them. Read your lines aloud often so they flow smoothly.

DURING THE PERFORMANCE

- **Keep your script away from your face but high enough to read:** If you cover your face with your script, you block your voice from the audience. If you have your script too low, you need to tip your head down farther to read it and the audience won't be able to hear you.

- **Use eye contact:** Good Reader's Theater performers look at the audience as much as they look at their scripts. If you look down, the sound of your voice goes down to the script and not out to the audience.

- **Speak clearly:** Make sure you are loud enough. Say all your words carefully. Be sure not to read too quickly. Remember, if you feel nervous, you may start to speak faster than usual.

- **Use facial expressions and gestures:** Your facial expressions and gestures (hand movements) help the audience know how your character is feeling. If your character is happy, smile. If your character is angry, cross your arms and be sure not to smile.

- **Have fun:** It's okay if you feel nervous. If you make a mistake, just try to relax and keep going. Reader's Theater is meant to be fun for the actors and the audience!

Cast of Characters

NARRATOR 1

NARRATOR 2

NARRATOR 3

READER 1:
Elbridge Gerry, William Paterson,
Edmund Randolph

READER 2:
Charles Pickney, Mercy Otis Warren

READER 3:
Gunning Bedford, Ben Franklin,
Alexander Hamilton

ROGER SHERMAN

ALL:
everyone except sound

SOUND:
This part has no lines. The person in this role
is in charge of the sound effects.
Find the sound effects for this script at
www.lerneresource.com.

The Script

NARRATOR 1: The year was 1787. The Revolutionary War was over. The Americans had won this war against Britain. Thirteen former British colonies broke free of Britain. They declared themselves the United States of America.

NARRATOR 2: In May, delegates from nearly all the thirteen states had come to Philadelphia, Pennsylvania. They headed to the Pennsylvania State House for an important meeting called a convention.

NARRATOR 3: A few delegates—such as George Washington and Benjamin Franklin—were famous. Seventeen more men were coming. Most had to ride for hundreds of miles on horseback or in carriages.

NARRATOR 1: The delegates met in the East Room of the State House. George Washington sat in a special chair. He had been the leader of the army during the Revolutionary War. People trusted him. The members elected him to be president of the convention.

NARRATOR 2: By 1787, the new country was in trouble. Congress ran the country. But rules put limits on how much power Congress had. Every state had to approve any changes to the rules.

NARRATOR 3: Because of these rules, Congress did not have enough money or power to govern strongly. The states' leaders gathered in Philadelphia to solve these problems.

Next Page — **NARRATOR 1**

NARRATOR 1: Some delegates planned to improve the rules. Others wanted to write a new set of rules. Edmund Randolph from Virginia had many ideas. These ideas were called the Virginia Plan.

READER 1 (as Edmund Randolph): My plan calls for a new type of government. There would be a president, a national court system, and a congress to make laws. Congress would have two parts—the House of Representatives and the Senate.

READER 2 (as Charles Pinckney): Would the president act like a king? Who would elect him? How long should he serve?

READER 3 (as Alexander Hamilton): I think the president should serve for life.

READER 2 (as Pinckney): Does the plan get rid of state governments?

NARRATOR 2: The delegates began to argue. At the time, each state had one vote in Congress. Under the new plan, things would be different. The number of votes each state had would be based on how many people lived in that state.

NARRATOR 3: The small states had fewer people than the big states. They were afraid the big states would run the country.

Next Page — **NARRATOR 1**

NARRATOR 1: The small states had a different plan. They called it the New Jersey Plan. Congress would only have one group of representatives. The states would keep their equal number of votes.

NARRATOR 2: Most of the delegates did not like the New Jersey Plan. They thought the Virginia Plan would work better. But they wanted to make changes to it. Elbridge Gerry from Massachusetts didn't like one part of the Virginia Plan.

READER 1 (as Elbridge Gerry): I do not want ordinary people to vote for members of the House of Representatives. People have the wildest ideas of government.

NARRATOR 3: The delegates could not go home until their work was done. They would have to stay in Philadelphia all summer.

NARRATOR 1: By June, the weather was very hot. The men wore wool coats, thick stockings, and heavy shoes. Many also wore itchy powdered wigs. Big black flies buzzed around the East Room. The heat made the flies worse.

SOUND: [Flies buzzing]

NARRATOR 2: When the delegates went for a walk, they often passed the Walnut Street Prison. The prisoners begged them for money. Sometimes the prisoners called them names.

Next Page — **ALL**

ALL (as prisoners): Boo! Go away!

NARRATOR 3: The members talked and voted. But they could not answer the biggest question. Should the large states send more representatives to Congress than the small states?

READER 1 (as William Paterson): Maybe the nation should have thirteen states the same size.

READER 2 (as Pinckney): Or divide the country into four equal parts.

NARRATOR 1: No one thought much of these ideas. Day after day, everyone argued. The small states were angry at the large states. Gunning Bedford from the tiny state of Delaware spoke up.

READER 3 (as Gunning Bedford): I do not trust you gentlemen! The large states cannot take all the power. They will crush the small states.

NARRATOR 2: Would they ever find a way to agree?

NARRATOR 3: The delegates took a break for the Fourth of July. Church bells rang, and fireworks exploded all across the country.

SOUND: [Church bells]

Next Page — **NARRATOR 1**

NARRATOR 1: Families watched the fireworks light up the summer sky.

SOUND: [Fireworks]

NARRATOR 2: The delegates were in a bad mood after the holiday. They were tired of arguing. Benjamin Franklin was worried that members would quit.

READER 3 (as Benjamin Franklin): None of you can get everything you want.

NARRATOR 3: Roger Sherman from Connecticut came up with a new plan. It included parts of both the Virginia and New Jersey plans.

ROGER SHERMAN: In the Connecticut Plan, citizens would elect members of the House of Representatives. The number of members would be based on the population of the state. Each state would send two representatives to the Senate. Members of the Senate would be chosen by the state governments.

NARRATOR 1: Finally, the delegates had a plan they could agree on.

ALL (as delegates): Agreed!

NARRATOR 2: The Connecticut Plan became known as the Great Compromise. A small group formed to write a draft of the new plan, which came to be called the Constitution. The rest of the delegates took a vacation.

Next Page — **NARRATOR 3**

NARRATOR 3: George Washington visited Valley Forge, north of Philadelphia. His army had camped there during the Revolutionary War. Crops grew in the fields where the soldiers once slept. Washington stayed with friends. He decided to go fishing for trout.

NARRATOR 1: The convention met again. This time, members looked at printed copies of the Constitution. Their work was not done yet.

ROGER SHERMAN: The president will be elected by people called electors. Voters in each state would choose these electors. The president will serve for four years. If he becomes sick, the vice president will take over.

READER 3 (as Alexander Hamilton): Congress can make changes to our laws when it needs to. We will call these changes amendments.

NARRATOR 2: The Constitution grew longer. The members got new copies with all their changes. They read the inspiring words at the beginning.

ALL: We the People of the United States, in Order to form a more perfect Union . . .

NARRATOR 3: On September 17, 1787, the Constitution was finished. Thirty-nine delegates signed it. Benjamin Franklin pointed to George Washington's chair.

READER 3 (as Benjamin Franklin): I've wondered if the sun carved on the back is rising or setting. Now I know it is a rising sun.

Next Page — **NARRATOR 1**

NARRATOR 1: A rising sun meant hope for the country's future. But the delegates still weren't done. The states had to vote on the Constitution. At least nine states had to approve it. If not, there would be no new government.

NARRATOR 2: Newspapers printed copies of the Constitution. People read it and argued about it. Some thought the new government would be too powerful.

NARRATOR 3: Mercy Otis Warren was from Massachusetts. She spoke against the Constitution.

READER 2 (as Mercy Otis Warren): The president will be too much like a king.

NARRATOR 1: Delaware was the first state to approve the Constitution. New Jersey, Pennsylvania, Georgia, and Connecticut followed. Slowly, more states voted yes. On June 21, 1788, New Hampshire became the ninth state to vote yes. The United States had a new Constitution.

NARRATOR 2: July 4, 1788, was another Independence Day. People were happy about the new U.S. Constitution. In Philadelphia, cannons boomed.

SOUND: [Cannon]

NARRATOR 3: Soldiers marched down the streets. Crowds cheered at a huge copy of the Constitution. It was on a float pulled by six horses.

SOUND: [Cheering crowd]

Next Page — **NARRATOR 2**

NARRATOR 2: In 1789, George Washington became the first U.S. president.

NARRATOR 1: The United States of America had a brand-new government. It was not like that of any other country. The Constitution would guide the United States through good times and bad. It was a new day for the country.

ALL: The End

Pronunciation Guide

congress: CON-grehs
constitution: con-stih-TOO-shun

convention: con-VEN-shuhn
delegate: DEHL-eh-geht

Glossary

citizen: a person who is protected by a government

Congress: the group that makes laws for the United States. In modern times, members of the U.S. Senate and the House of Representatives make up the U.S. Congress.

constitution: a document that explains the powers and duties of the government

convention: a meeting of people for a common purpose

delegate: a person who represents others at a meeting. The delegates to the Constitutional Convention represented their states.

elect: to choose for office by voting

float: a decorated scene mounted on wheels and pulled in a parade

representative: a person acting for a group of people

Valley Forge: a place eighteen miles from Philadelphia where General George Washington's troops camped during the harsh winter of 1777–1778

Selected Bibliography

BOOKS

Collier, Christopher, and James Lincoln. *Decision in Philadelphia: The Constitution Convention of 1787.* New York: Random, 1986.

Peters, William. *A More Perfect Union: The Making of the United States Constitution.* New York: Crown, 1987.

Peterson, Merrill D. *James Madison: A Biography in His Own Words, Vol. I.* New York: Newsweek, 1974.

Stewart, David O. *The Summer of 1787: The Men Who Invented the Constitution.* New York: Simon & Schuster, 2007.

WEBSITES

Annenberg Center for Education & Outreach. "Founders: Delegates to the Constitutional Convention." National Constitution Center. 2010. http://constitutioncenter.org/ncc_edu_Founders.aspx (January 15, 2010).

Ashbrook Center for Public Affairs. "Notes of Debates in the Federal Convention of 1787 by James Madison." Teaching American History.org. 2008. http://teachingamericanhistory.org/convention/debates (January 15, 2010).

Further Reading and Websites

BOOKS

Catrow, David. *We the Kids: The Preamble to the Constitution of the United States.* New York: Dial, 2002.
Cartoons tell the story of the first part of the Constitution, known as the preamble, and what it means.

Fritz, Jean. *Shh! We're Writing the Constitution*. New York: Putnam, 1997.
This book is filled with fun, interesting facts about the Founding Fathers and the convention.

Mitchell, Barbara. *Father of the Constitution: A Story about James Madison*. Minneapolis: Millbrook Press, 2004.
James Madison was an important member of the Constitutional Convention. This book shows how he helped shape our nation.

Ransom, Candice. *George Washington*. Minneapolis: Lerner Publications Company, 2002.
Learn more about the life story of the first U.S. president.

Ransom, Candice. *Who Wrote the U.S. Constitution?* Minneapolis: Lerner Publications Company, 2011.
In this book, find the answers to six key questions about the 1787 convention and the writing of the Constitution.

WEBSITES

Constitution Facts
http://www.constitutionfacts.com
Fun facts about the Constitution and the Founding Fathers are available at this site.

The Constitution for Kids
http://www.usconstitution.net/constkidsK.html
This site gives basic facts about the Constitution, the Bill of Rights, and the amendments.

The Preamble Scramble
http://www.texaslre.org/preamble_intro.html
Help the Founding Fathers put the preamble to the Constitution in the right order.

Dear Teachers and Librarians,

Congratulations on bringing Reader's Theater to your students! Reader's Theater is an excellent way for your students to develop their reading fluency. Phrasing and inflection, two important reading skills, are at the heart of Reader's Theater. Students also develop public speaking skills such as volume, pacing, and facial expression.

The traditional format of Reader's Theater is very simple. There really is no right or wrong way to do it. By following these few tips, you and your students will be ready to explore the world of Reader's Theater.

EQUIPMENT

Location: A theater or gymnasium is a fine place for a Reader's Theater performance, but staging the performance in the classroom works well too.

Scripts: Each reader will need a copy of the script. Scripts that are individually printed should be bound into binders that allow the readers to turn the pages easily. Printable scripts for all the books in this series are available at www.lerneresource.com.

Music Stands: Music stands are very helpful for the readers to set their scripts on.

Costumes: Traditional Reader's Theater does not use costumes. Dressing uniformly, such as all wearing the same color shirt, will give a group a polished look. Specific costume pieces can be used when a reader is performing multiple roles. They help the audience follow the story.

Props: Props are optional. If necessary, readers may mime or gesture to convey objects that are important to the story. Props can be used much like a costume piece to identify different characters performed by one reader. Prop suggestions for each story are available at www.lerneresource.com.

Background and Sound Effects: These aren't essential, but they can add to the fun of Reader's Theater. Customized backgrounds for each story in this series and sound effects corresponding to the scripts are available at www.lerneresource.com. You will need a screen or electronic whiteboard for the background. You will need a computer with speakers to play the sound effects.

PERFORMANCE

Staging: Readers usually face the audience in a straight line or a semicircle. If the readers are using music stands, the stands should be raised chest high. A stand should not block a reader's mouth or face, but it should allow for the reader to read without looking down too much. The main character is usually placed in the center. The narrator is on the end. In the case of multiple narrators, place one narrator on each end.

Reading: Reader's Theater scripts do not need to be memorized. However, the readers should be familiar enough with the script to maintain a fair amount of eye contact with the audience. Encourage readers to act with their voices by reading with inflection and emotion.

Blocking (stage movement): For traditional Reader's Theater, there are no blocking cues to follow. You may want to have the students turn the pages simultaneously. Some groups prefer that readers sit or turn their back to the audience when their characters are "offstage" or have left a scene. Some groups will have their readers move about the stage, script in hand, to interact with the other readers. The choice is up to you.

Overture and Curtain Call: Before the performance, a member of the group should announce the title and the author of the piece. At the end of the performance, all readers step in front of their music stands, stand in a line, grasp hands, and bow in unison.

Please visit www.lerneresource.com for printable scripts, prop suggestions, sound effects, a background image that can be projected on a screen or electronic whiteboard, a Reader's Theater teacher's guide, and reading-level information for all roles.